The Berenstain Bears

Think of Those in Need

Almost all bears discover,
in a little while,
that what they've outgrown
makes quite a pile.

A First Time Book®

Copyright © 1999 by Berenstain Enterprises, Inc. All rights reserved under International
and Pan-American Copyright Conventions. Published in the United States by
Random House, Inc., New York, and simultaneously in Canada by
Random House of Canada Limited, Toronto.
www.randomhouse.com/kids   www.berenstainbears.com
Library of Congress Cataloging-in-Publication Data: Berenstain, Stan, 1923–
The Berenstain Bears Think of Those in Need / Stan and Jan Berenstain.
p. cm. – (A first time book)
SUMMARY: When Mama Bear decides that the family has accumulated too many old toys, books,
and games, they sort through all their extra stuff and take it to the Old Bears' Home,
the Beartown Young Cubs Hospital, and the Bears Who Care store.
ISBN 0-679-88957-4 (trade) — ISBN 0-679-98957-9 (lib. bdg.)
[1. Charity—Fiction. 2. Bears—Fiction.] I. Berenstain, Jan, 1923– . II. Title.
III. Series: Berenstain, Stan, 1923–   First time books. PZ7.B4483Bat 1999
[E]–dc21 98-54215
Printed in the United States of America 10 9 8 7 6 5 4 3 2 1

The Berenstain Bears

Think of Those in Need

Stan & Jan Berenstain

Random House 🏠 New York

The Bear family enjoyed the good
things in life as much as anyone else.
They enjoyed good food and good
times.

They enjoyed a snug tree house and a comfortable chair before a crackling fire.

They enjoyed books and music,

toys and games,

quilts and cuckoo clocks.

But sometimes it seemed, especially to Mama, that perhaps the Bears were enjoying too much of a good thing. It was also clear to Mama, as she managed the tree house, that they had a problem—a problem that came under the heading of *Too Much Stuff*.

Too much stuff in the closets...

too much stuff in the drawers...

too much stuff in
the basement...

too much stuff in the attic...
There was too much stuff
everywhere.

It all made Mama a little
uneasy. It was beginning to
be a worry.

Papa thought there was a "too much stuff" problem, too. But he was more annoyed than worried—annoyed about a Fast Wheels car that Brother had left on the stairs and about a squeaky duck that Sister had left in the bathtub.

SQUEAK!

But there was much more on Mama's mind than Fast Wheels cars and squeaky ducks. What was beginning to worry her was that they had so much, while some others had so little.

And as sometimes happens with a worry,
when you go to bed, it can turn into a nightmare.
That's what happened to Mama.

One night she dreamed that all their stuff came to life and poured out of every drawer and closet and nook and cranny in the tree house, chanting, "Too much stuff! Too much stuff!"

"What's the matter?" asked Papa when Mama woke up screaming.

"It was just a dream, my dear," Mama said. But though it was just a dream, she knew what she had to do.

The next morning, at breakfast, she made an announcement.

"This family," she said firmly, "has altogether too much stuff. It's time to get rid of some of it."

"Stuff?" said Brother. "What sort of stuff?"

"Stuff like dolls with no heads," Mama said, "broken airplane models, old puzzles, games that nobody plays..."

"And Fast Wheels cars on the stairs and squeaky ducks in the bathtub," chimed in Papa.

"Now wait a minute," protested Sister. "That's all *our* stuff. What about some of *your* stuff?"

"*My* stuff?" said Papa. "Like what?"

"Like your seventeen fishing rods," said Brother.

"And the zillions of old fishing magazines you have stacked up in the attic," added Sister.

"But those are all valuable collectibles!" said Papa.
Mama groaned.

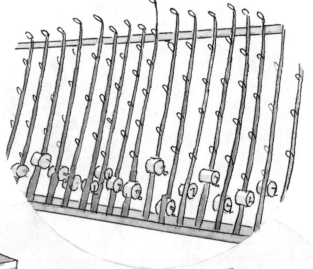

"Look who's groaning!" said Papa. "What about those shelves and shelves of old cookbooks you never look at and those bits of yarn and cloth you're never going to use?"

"All right," agreed Mama. "I guess we all have a lot of things we don't really need. That's just my point. What should we do with it all?"

The Bear family thought for a moment.
"Hey!" said Brother. "Let's have a yard sale and make a fortune."
"Yeah! Great idea!" agreed Sister and Papa.
But that was not what Mama had in mind. She had been thinking more and more about all those folks who had so little. Especially with Christmas coming on.
But what could the Bear family do?
Mama already had a plan in mind.

First, she had Papa and the cubs go through all their stuff and make three piles. In one pile were things like old board games and puzzles. In another, all their forgotten but still good toys and sporting goods. And in another, clothes and furniture, extra cookbooks and unused fishing rods.

When the Bears piled everything into the car, there was hardly enough room left for them.

"Where are we going?" asked Sister. "First stop," said Mama, "is the Old Bears' Home."

The Old Bears' Home was where older bears went to live when they needed help taking care of themselves. Nurses and doctors looked after them and made sure they were in good health. But sometimes the older bears got a little lonely and bored. They liked visitors and things to do.

That was part of Mama's plan. When the family arrived at the Old Bears' Home, they handed out their games and puzzles to the older bears and then sat down to play games and do puzzles with them.

At first, Brother and
Sister were a little shy and
embarrassed. The older bears
were just so old! But after a
while, they got over it. The
bears in the home weren't any
older than their neighbor Miz
McGrizz, and she was okay.

Soon they were having a fine
time. And so were the older
bears. They were all sorry
when it was time to leave.

Their next stop was the Beartown Young Cubs Hospital. Brother and Sister knew about the hospital. Brother had gone there to get his ankle x-rayed the time they thought it was broken. And Sister had come along to watch.

The Bears dropped off their load of used toys. They were welcome. The hospital workers said the toys would be given out at the hospital Christmas party. On their way out, they saw a young bear in a wheelchair with his leg in a big cast. They were glad they had brought the toys. He looked as if he could use some cheering up.

Their last stop was the Beartown Bears Who Care store. This was a store that sold things to raise money for needy bears—bears who needed warm clothes and good food. The store was run by bears who wore uniforms and often played in a band in front of the store.

The Bears lugged all their old clothes and furniture and stuff into the store. On the way, they stopped to sing a few Christmas carols with the band.

There was a big iron pot out on the sidewalk for collecting money for the needy. Papa gave Sister a dollar to put in it.

They headed home with warm feelings about what they had done.

As they drove along, they passed the lighted windows of the Beartown Department Store. They were beautifully decorated for Christmas. There was window after window of new toys and games, new things for the house, and the very latest thing in fishing poles.

But the members of the Bear family were so filled with special thoughts about helping others that they hardly noticed the wonderful things in the windows...

except maybe out of the corners of their eyes.

The Berenstain Bears Present

  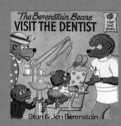   

     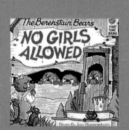

www.randomhouse.com/kids
www.berenstainbears.com

$3.25 U.S. $4.25 CAN.

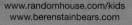
0-375-80888-4